D0114206

The Cave Challenge

Bear Grylls

The Cave Challenge

Bear Grylls
Illustrated by Emma McCann

Bear Grylls

First American Edition 2019
Kane Miller, A Division of EDC Publishing

First published in Great Britain in 2018 by Bear Grylls, an imprint
of Bonnier Zaffre, a Bonnier Publishing Company
Text and illustrations copyright © Bear Grylls Ventures, 2018
Illustrations by Emma McCann

For information contact:
Kane Miller, A Division of EDC Publishing
PO Box 470663
Tulsa, OK 74147-0663
www.kanemiller.com
www.edcpub.com
www.usbornebooksandmore.com

Library of Congress Control Number: 2018958213

Manufactured by Regent Publishing Services, Hong Kong
Printed May 2019 in ShenZhen, Guangdong, China

1 2 3 4 5 6 7 8 9 10

ISBN: 978-1-68464-019-5

*To the young survivor
reading this book for the first time.
May your eyes always be wide open
to adventure, and your heart full
of courage and determination to
see your dreams through.*

1

THE MILLION DOLLAR QUESTION

Harry slunk along the path towards the clearing, feeling annoyed.

He'd just come from the construction challenge, where everyone had been building a cart from bits of old junk. The wheels had been stiff, so Evie had squirted oil on them ... and on Harry's leg.

His jeans were *ruined.*

Harry bitterly ran through the list of Bad Things That Had Happened that day. First, he had spilled mayo on his Chimp Skinny jeans. He loved his Chimp Skinnys; they'd been brand-new. He was really upset with himself for not being more careful. He'd washed them as best he could, and missed out on eating his lunch with the others.

Harry had changed into a spare pair of jeans before the construction challenge. They weren't Chimps, only Fully Leaded, but they still looked pretty good.

But Evie had gotten oil on them!

He'd never be able to wash that off.

Harry hardly dared to look at the damage, but he guessed he had to. He had to know how bad it really was.

The oil stain was thick and black, all across one leg.

Harry always avoided getting dirty, and took extra care of his clothes and appearance. It was a *calamity*.

No one else at camp cared. Well, Evie had given him some silly compass to try to make up for the oil. She seemed to think there was something special about it, but it was just a compass. It wasn't going to make up for a ruined pair of jeans.

So Harry was heading back to change clothes *again*.

The next activity was Frisbee team. Harry had deliberately chosen it because it was indoors, so he could wear his new white sneakers and white Croc Byte T-shirt. He knew they looked great together because he'd planned all his outfits at home in front of the mirror. This one made him look like his favorite basketball player.

"Hey, Harry!"

Harry heard his name being called, but he didn't feel like talking to anyone right now. He wasn't in the mood. He kept walking.

"Harry! Wait up!"

Harry sighed and turned around.

"Hi, guys."

"Harry, where are you going?"

Charlie and Joe fell in on either side of Harry, smiling and happy.

"I was just going to get changed for Frisbee team," Harry said.

"Great – we're heading to the tent too," said Joe.

"Hey, have you read about this guy who didn't realize he'd won a million dollars?" Charlie said. "Can you imagine it? He didn't realize! What would *you* do if you accidentally won a million dollars?"

Before Harry could say anything, Joe interrupted.

"I'd invent this thing like a global map, see? And it would always tell you exactly where you were, and how to get to where you want to be."

Harry had to smile. Joe's total lack of sense of direction was legendary.

"Don't we already have that?" Harry said grumpily. "It's … well. It's GPS. Satellite navigation. It's already been invented."

"Yeah, but mine would know every single path and track and everything. And … wait for it! It would project onto your eyes, so you'd literally know where you were, every single second."

"I'd use a million dollars to invent the most totally cool games ever," Charlie decided. "They'd be totally immersive and they'd interact with real things too, so that you could make anything be fun. Like, we could shoot each other with laser guns in the game, and hide behind that tree there in real life."

"Maybe you two could work together," Harry suggested. "GPS … games, it's all electronics."

The other two boys looked at each other thoughtfully.

"Charlie, do you want to put your

games on my GPS?" Joe said.

"Nah," Charlie said scornfully. "But if you want, I can invent a GPS that plays games ..."

They carried on arguing, which meant Harry got out of having to answer the question.

What would I do with one million dollars? he thought, looking at the massive oil stain on his Fully Leaded jeans. Easy. He'd invent a special high-tech fabric that dirt could never stick to.

Harry glanced at his watch. They were going to be late if they didn't move it. And he still needed to get changed.

"Guys, gotta go!"

2

FRISBEE FROLICS

Harry had timed his leap perfectly. As the Frisbee curved through the air into his hands, he felt a thrill of satisfaction as his fingers closed around the spinning plastic.

Half a second later his feet hit the ground. *Splat!* He'd landed right in the middle of a muddy puddle. Dirty water splashed onto his white socks, white sneakers and light-gray cargo shorts.

They were supposed to have played in the gym, where it was nice and dry and clean. That was why he had chosen Frisbee team. But the gym had been accidentally double booked and Frisbee team had to go outside onto the soccer field.

The damp and muddy soccer field.

Harry stared at his feet in horror, too distracted to notice someone snatching the Frisbee from his hand.

"Hey!" he protested.

"Ha!" The girl who had snatched it grinned, and flung it on to another teammate.

This was Frisbee team. You had to get the Frisbee into the other team's goal. You couldn't run with the Frisbee, you could only throw it. You could jump and catch the Frisbee if it was flying, or knock it out of the air with your hand or your body. And you could snatch it away from someone who had just caught it, as long as you did it within one second.

Which the girl on the other team had done.

"Harry!" George shouted in frustration. He had been in the perfect position for Harry to pass to him.

Now the Frisbee was soaring into the goal. The Yellow team cheered while the Red team groaned and stared at Harry.

The ref blew her whistle.

"End of quarter, time to switch out!" she called.

The teams had five players each, but there were more than ten people playing. So, they switched in and out at the end of each quarter, to give everyone a turn. It was Harry's turn to switch out.

Probably best, he thought bitterly. *Yet another activity ruined.*

He plonked himself down on a bench and glared at his spattered sneakers.

Harry watched glumly from the bench as the next quarter started. He checked his pockets to see if he had anything to wipe the mud off. But all he pulled out was the compass that Evie had given him.

Huh?

That was weird. He was sure he had left it in his jeans in the tent. He must have been in such a rush that he'd picked it up again without thinking.

Harry studied it again. He still didn't see what Evie thought was special about it. It was just a regular compass – dial, needle ... and *five* directions!

As if that wasn't strange enough, the needle started spinning around and around.

Harry stared. What was the point of a compass with five directions and a broken needle?

He shoved it back into his pocket and stood up. Some of his teammates who were waiting for their next turn were messing around on the playground near the field. It had an all-weather surface, so Harry guessed he could join in and not get his sneakers any more muddy, at least.

Harry balanced on the rolling log for a while before moving on to the rope swing. He gripped the rope between his hands and knees and swung himself out into midair…

Out of nowhere, a wall of solid rock came zooming straight at him.

"Aargh!"

Harry landed so hard on the rock that he let go of the rope. He turned around and saw that there was nothing behind him. He was right on the edge of a narrow stone ledge, above a lake of blue water. Harry waved his arms in circles, trying to regain his balance until at last he was standing up straight again.

He stared around in amazement.

Camp had vanished. The soccer field, the playground, his friends – all gone.

He looked up. His ledge was almost at the bottom of a giant stone pit. The water was ten feet below him, so clear that Harry could easily see the rocky bed. As he stared, a shoal of fish swam lazily beneath him.

The pit was roughly circular, about sixty feet wide and deep. Its stone sides were almost hidden behind curtains of vines and creepers. There was a vast overhang all around the top, so that even if Harry could climb up there, it would be impossible to climb out.

And it was *incredibly* hot and humid.

The ledge was only ten or twelve feet long. Harry moved up and down it, looking everywhere for a way up or out.

But he soon saw there *was* no way out. He was stuck.

"Hi, there!"

A man's voice echoed around the stone pit.

Harry's head whipped around.

3

CAVEMAN

The man stood on some rocks a few feet away, just above water level. He had come out of a cave that Harry hadn't noticed at first. Harry had thought it was just a crack in the rock.

The man was wearing red coveralls and a battered helmet with a light on the front. The outfit made Harry think of miners, except that the man also had a backpack slung onto his back.

"There's a way out," the man called, "but you need to come over here."

"How?" Harry asked in frustration. "I can't see any way down."

The man smiled and pointed at the wall of vegetation that covered the stone behind Harry.

"You can use one of those vines behind you to swing over." He held a thumb up. "Find one that's about as thick as my thumb, and that's green and alive, not brown and dead. It needs to be strong and flexible."

"Um – okay."

Harry started to feel through the vines at the end of the ledge nearest to the man.

Some of the vines were too thin for him to get a good grip on. Some looked fine but snapped when he tugged on them. Eventually he had one about the right thickness and gave it a tug to test it.

"How's this –" he started to call, and flinched as a bunch of leaves and bugs fell down on him from above. He flicked off the bugs, shook his head, and ran his fingers through his hair. His hair that he spent ages on every morning.

"Are you okay, buddy?" the man called.

Harry glowered down at himself. The debris had left dirty smudges on his white T-shirt, and his hair was probably full of disgusting stuff. Yuck.

"No," he muttered. Then, so the man could hear him, "Fine, thanks."

"Great. And that vine looks like a good one. Swing yourself over."

Harry nervously gripped the vine. He had seen people swinging on vines in movies, but never in real life. But he knew he couldn't stay on this ledge forever. Besides, if the vine snapped then the worst that could happen would be he fell into the lake. At least it would be a soft landing.

Harry tightened his grip and swung himself out into space.

The rocky pit and the blue water blurred past his eyes. The man came shooting towards him on a collision course. Harry had a vision of them both ending up in the water, but the man caught him just in time.

"Well done!" he said, smiling. "You can let go of the vine now, champ."

Harry and the man were standing

together on the rocks. The entrance to the cave was a jagged, mostly vertical crack, a bit taller than the man.

"You did it!" the man said cheerfully. "I'm Bear," he said, putting his hand out.

"I'm Harry."

"Well, Harry, I'm going to guide you out of here."

Harry looked around. *"Where* are we? It's so hot!"

"Well, up there on the surface, it's all jungle. We're in a cenote."

The word sounded like "sin-o-tee." Harry had never heard it before.

"What's one of those?"

"Sometimes you get a really big cave underground, very close to the surface. The roof is so thin that it collapses, and the cave becomes a pit, like this. I got here because I've been exploring this network of caves." The man waved a hand at the entrance behind him.

"You said there's no other way out," said Harry.

The man nodded.

"We'll have to retrace my steps to find our way back to the surface. Are you ready for some real adventure?"

"Sure," Harry said immediately, with a relieved smile. He already knew he would be clueless in a place like this. He needed a guide more than anything, and Bear looked like a good guy.

Bear grinned.

"Okay, I'd better kit you out." He looked Harry up and down with a smile. "What you've got on looks pretty nice."

"Yeah? It's Croc Byte," said Harry, pleased Bear thought he looked good, despite the mud and everything.

"But," said Bear, "I'm afraid it's not going to help you much where we're going." He swung his backpack down to the ground and started to rummage through it.

Harry's smile froze as he took in the state of Bear's coveralls for the first time.

"Uh – will it be dirty?" he asked.

"Filthy!" Bear smiled. "Mud and slime everywhere. Are you okay with that?"

Harry scowled. What could he say? *No thanks, I'll just sit here until someone cleans the caves up for me?* That would be ridiculous.

But he hated the idea of getting filthy. He would never usually sign up for anything that meant he would trash his clothes or look silly.

"I guess…" he said glumly.

"That's the right spirit, Harry," Bear said cheerfully. "You might not get a choice about having to be a survivor, but you always get a choice about how you think about it. If you can think positively then your body finds it a whole lot easier to follow."

Bear pulled another pair of coveralls out of his backpack. They were like the ones he was wearing, but blue, and crisp and brand-new. They looked fresh from the store. Harry breathed a sigh of relief. Maybe he could get away with not getting too messed up.

"You can wear these over what you've already got on. They're tough and rugged. Some of the rocks in there are sharp, and wet skin swells and damages very easily, which means you could pick up cuts and bruises that will get infected. These will protect you."

"So – they're not going to keep me dry?" Harry checked.

"Sorry, champ. Nothing will keep you dry down here. But at least the coveralls can keep you a bit safer when you do get wet."

While Harry pulled the coveralls on, Bear pulled out another helmet, and a pair of scuffed, well-used boots.

"These are vital too. Your head needs protection, and the boots will give you a grip on wet surfaces, as well as ankle support."

Harry was tempted to sniff the boots first and make sure they were clean inside, but Bear was looking. He laced them up while Bear took his white sneakers and stowed them in his backpack.

Harry looked at the helmet. It was really going to mess his hair up. But before he could say anything Bear had placed it on his head and was adjusting the straps so that it was a perfect fit. Like Bear's helmet, it had an LED light fixed to the front of it, and a chin strap to hold it in place.

"All ready to go?" Bear asked.

"I suppose." Harry decided not to say anything about the helmet just then. He'd take it off later.

They turned their headlights on, and Bear led the way into the darkness.

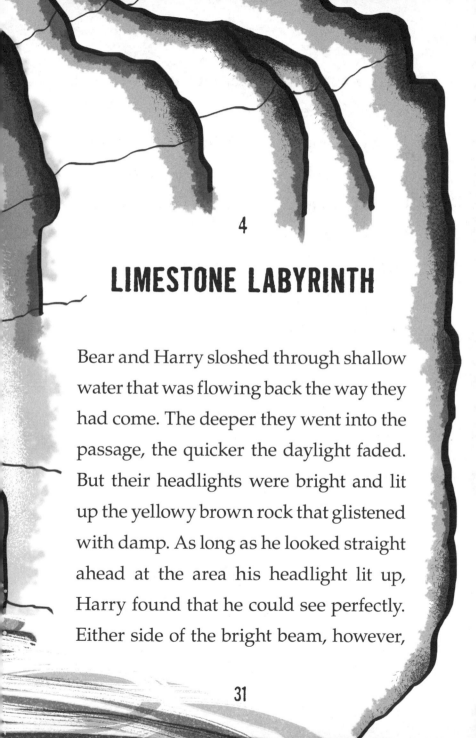

4

LIMESTONE LABYRINTH

Bear and Harry sloshed through shallow water that was flowing back the way they had come. The deeper they went into the passage, the quicker the daylight faded. But their headlights were bright and lit up the yellowy brown rock that glistened with damp. As long as he looked straight ahead at the area his headlight lit up, Harry found that he could see perfectly. Either side of the bright beam, however, there was nothing but darkness.

The farther they walked, the more Harry thought about the walls of the passage. They were covered in smooth bumps, like the roof of your mouth. Harry shuddered. It was like being swallowed by a giant throat.

If Harry had thought the air outside the cave was hot, in here it was hotter. The farther they went, the warmer the air became. Soon, it felt like warm, wet blankets being stuffed into his mouth.

"It's boiling!" Harry said.

"And humid too," Bear replied, ahead of him. "There's a lot of moisture in the air, which means our sweat can't evaporate, so we don't cool down. But we're still losing water. So we'll be stopping for regular water breaks."

Harry looked down at the stream.

"At least there's plenty of water here!"

"There certainly is!" Bear agreed. "These caves wouldn't be here without it. There are hundreds of miles of caves and tunnels down here, all of them eroded by water over hundreds of thousands of years."

"So why did the caves just stop back at the cenote?" Harry asked. "There was only one way in or out."

"Only one way in and out for us," Bear pointed out, "but the water can go its own way."

"Ah-h-h." It dawned on Harry. "So there might be more caves underwater, right?"

"Got it in one. Some caves you can only explore with air tanks and wetsuits

– but let's keep that for another day, shall we?"

The tunnel soon began to shrink. Bear had to duck to a half crouch, half crawl. Salty sweat trickled down Harry's forehead and ran into his eyes. It was gross and it stung. He blinked, hard. He could feel his hair plastered to his head. Yuck. Harry undid his helmet strap and took it off, and the light from his helmet swung all around the tunnel.

Bear immediately said, "Whoa!"

"I'm just sorting my hair," Harry explained. "The helmet's so hot, and it's squashing my hair down."

"That's fine, but we don't move until your helmet is back on," Bear said. "You don't realize how hard your head can hit solid rock. Just a normal walking pace could mean a nasty crack and a head wound."

Bear sounded serious. Harry could tell he wouldn't budge until he put the helmet back on. He slicked his hair back, out of his eyes, and put his helmet back on again. He thoughtlessly stood up straight – and immediately his head hit the rock ceiling with a dull "clonk."

"Whoa!"

Bear grinned.

"You see what I mean, buddy?"

Harry did. Okay, the helmet didn't look good, but at least it was keeping him from injuring himself. Even with the helmet on it had really hurt to bang his head against the rock. He crouched down like Bear as they moved forward.

After a few minutes they reached a junction where the tunnel split in two directions. The stream flowed out of the right-hand tunnel. Bear's headlight lit up a small pile of stones by the left-hand one.

"This way," Bear said, heading to the left. The new tunnel sloped upward a little, out of the stream. The walls were still damp, though. By now, Harry had learned that the walls were always damp.

Harry looked at the pile of stones as he clambered past it.

"Did you put those stones there?" he asked.

"Yes, I used them to mark my route on the way down. Your markers stand out if they're obviously man-made, like a pyramid of stones or the shape of an arrow. Anyone who sees them will know they've been put there for a reason."

The tunnel got larger again. They could move more easily, but they still weren't exactly walking. Everywhere they went, they had to climb and scramble and pick their way carefully. There wasn't a single smooth surface anywhere. *You could tell that this place had been carved out by nature*, Harry thought. Humans hadn't had a hand in it.

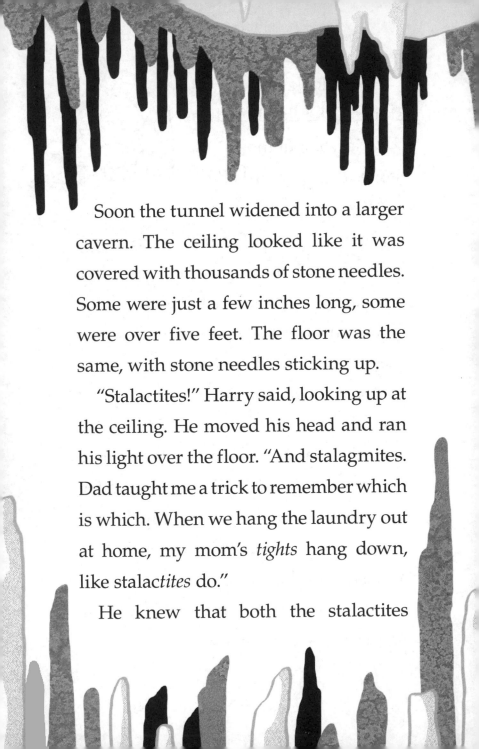

Soon the tunnel widened into a larger cavern. The ceiling looked like it was covered with thousands of stone needles. Some were just a few inches long, some were over five feet. The floor was the same, with stone needles sticking up.

"Stalactites!" Harry said, looking up at the ceiling. He moved his head and ran his light over the floor. "And stalagmites. Dad taught me a trick to remember which is which. When we hang the laundry out at home, my mom's *tights* hang down, like stalac*tites* do."

He knew that both the stalactites

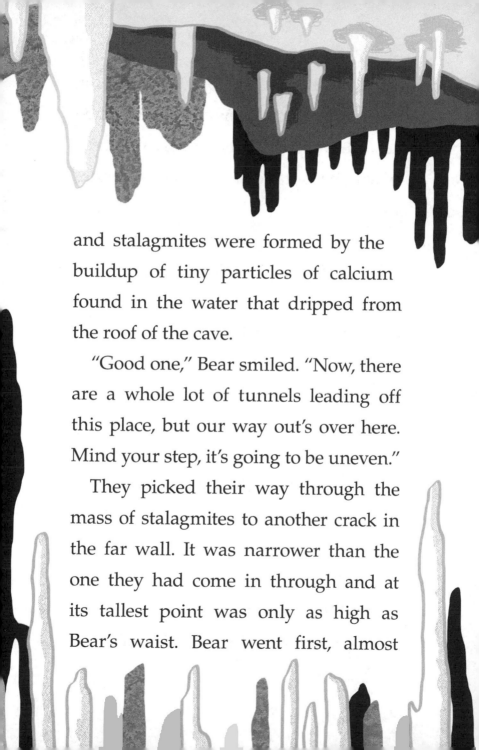

and stalagmites were formed by the buildup of tiny particles of calcium found in the water that dripped from the roof of the cave.

"Good one," Bear smiled. "Now, there are a whole lot of tunnels leading off this place, but our way out's over here. Mind your step, it's going to be uneven."

They picked their way through the mass of stalagmites to another crack in the far wall. It was narrower than the one they had come in through and at its tallest point was only as high as Bear's waist. Bear went first, almost

having to lie on his front to get into it.
Harry crouched down and watched
Bear disappear. After about a minute
he saw Bear stand up in a black, empty
space.

Bear called back to him. "Your turn!"

Harry found it easier than Bear had
because he was smaller. But whenever
he lifted his head to see where he was
going, his helmet clonked against the
rock again. His light reflected straight
back into his eyes from the rock in front
of him. When his chest pressed into the
rock, he could feel the dampness soaking
his coveralls. He tried not to think about
what he looked like now.

Then Harry felt space opening up
around him. He could stand up straight.
The dampness had soaked through the

coveralls and he could feel his T-shirt clinging to his chest. He was covered in dirt.

"We can take a breather here," Bear said. "We've earned it."

The air was full of the sound of rushing water, but Harry couldn't see what was causing it. That small little crack had brought them into a cavern that had to be thirty feet in all directions. Harry dragged his attention away from his grimy clothes, and moved his head around and up and down, to sweep the light beam around.

He looked up, and the circle of light fell onto a falling torrent of water.

A waterfall! It disappeared into a hole in the ground.

And next to the cascading water was something so ordinary it looked completely out of place.

A rope. It hung next to the fall and disappeared up into the dark.

"Is that the way out?" Harry asked warily.

"That's right," Bear said. "Straight up that fall."

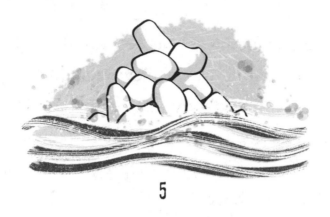

5

WATER OBSTACLE

Bear gave the rope a tug to check it.

"This got me down, and it'll get us up again. Are you any good at climbing?"

"Sure," Harry said truthfully. "I've been on the climbing wall a lot."

The wall at camp was one of his favorite activities. He loved the challenge of stretching out his hands and feet between the rubber grips and footholds. It was indoors, so he could wear his best stuff while he showed off his skills. He really felt he was achieving something, pushing his body up against gravity, and he knew he looked good doing it.

"That's good news, Harry," said Bear. "Can you handle a slope like this?"

"Um – sure. I think." Harry felt fairly confident. The slope wasn't completely vertical, just very steep. He guessed he could manage it. But the climbing wall at camp was clean and dry. It didn't have a waterfall tumbling down next to it.

"Take this. It's caving rope," Bear said, passing it to Harry to feel. "It's flexible and designed to shed water, so we can still get a grip on it. Try it."

Harry gave it a pull.

"Uh-huh," he said politely. Bear had been right that you could get a good grip on it. But it was covered with droplets of water from the waterfall's spray, and all that water went somewhere. Specifically, it trickled wetly over his fingers and wrists and down his sleeves. He couldn't wipe his hands without getting more dirty.

But at least he knew they had the right equipment.

They had a quick break, drinking some water from Bear's bottle and each eating an energy bar. Then Harry was first up the rope. Hundreds of tons of water roared by in the opposite direction. He made sure his boots were firmly planted with each step and hauled himself up

the rope, hand over hand. Pretty soon his arms were aching from all the effort. The fall drenched him in spray, but his coveralls protected him.

Eventually Harry climbed over the ledge at the top, where Bear had tied the rope to a stalagmite.

"I'm up!" he called, and settled back to wait for Bear. He rolled up his sleeves to cool himself down, and looked down at his coveralls. They were damp, but the sturdy material wasn't soaked through. *Neat piece of design*, Harry thought approvingly.

The rope went rigid as Bear climbed

up. While Harry waited, he flashed his headlight along the tunnel ahead. It was the first time that Harry was in the lead since they entered the caves. Beyond his light, there was nothing but pitch darkness. Just mile after mile of caves, he guessed.

The tunnel was narrow and twisty, so he would have to be careful where he put his feet. And they would be sharing it with the stream that was flowing rapidly downhill towards the waterfall.

"Why does everything bend so much?" he wondered as Bear clambered up to meet him. "Why doesn't the water wash the stone away in straight lines?"

"Great question! It's all limestone, but it's not all the same strength," Bear said as he reached the top. "Limestone is made from the remains of marine animals, like coral or shellfish. Over millions and millions of years their bodies leave calcium behind. It doesn't go in straight lines because living creatures don't go in straight lines. There might be other bits mixed up in it, or air bubbles trapped in it. The water just follows the lines of weakness."

Bear coiled the rope up and put it in his backpack. Together they set off again up the tunnel, picking their way over rocks and trying to stay out of the stream.

Soon they came to another of Bear's little marker piles. This one was below a hole in the ceiling that was about six feet above them.

"Up we go," Bear said.

He gave Harry a boost up to the next level, then climbed up behind. Harry tried to stand up, but his helmet clonked against the roof again. He had to squat. In fact, he had to lie almost on his front to go any farther. This bit wasn't much more than a crack.

"We'll have to go leopard style for a while," Bear said. "But don't worry, it gets bigger. I'll lead."

Bear took his backpack off and pushed it ahead of him. Then he slowly disappeared like a snake going into a hole, pulling himself along on his elbows.

Harry watched the soles of Bear's boots get farther away.

A couple of minutes later it was Harry's turn.

The crack really was narrow. Harry had pulled his sleeves back down again, but he could feel his elbows grinding into the limestone through the fabric.

For the first time, Harry started thinking about the millions of tons of rock above him. If even just a few rocks came down he could be blocked in here forever …

He told himself not to be silly. Bear had done this. He could too.

But it was a huge relief when he popped out into a larger chamber and could stand up again. Beyond his headlight beam, the chamber turned into a new tunnel, continuing onward. Bear grinned and handed Harry another energy bar and his water bottle.

"I think we've earned a break!"

Harry took a long drink. "What happens if we run out of water?" he asked.

"Well, this water around us has been filtered by miles of limestone," Bear said. "So it should be clean to drink if we need to."

Harry looked around at the glistening walls, and down at his clothes. Nothing looked clean.

"So, where did all this dirt come from then?"

"Most of it's limescale – dissolved calcium left behind by the water. Some of it will be silt left over from when the cave was flooded. Water coming straight out of the rock will be absolutely pure," Bear said. "But there's always a risk that algae growing in the damp might contaminate it, so we'd need to be careful how we collected the water. We'll drink from our own supplies for as long as we can."

Something caught Harry's eye right next to him in a pool.

A little pile of rocks was sticking up out of the water.

"Why did you put a marker underwater?" Harry asked.

"I didn't," Bear said, frowning. "I put them all where I could see them." Bear took a long hard look at the pile, then back at the crack they had come through.

"Wait here," he said, before disappearing.

A couple of minutes later he returned. His face was thoughtful.

"There must be a rainstorm on the surface, and it's all coming down here. The water's almost up to the ceiling back the way we came. And that pool there is the tunnel I came through the first time.

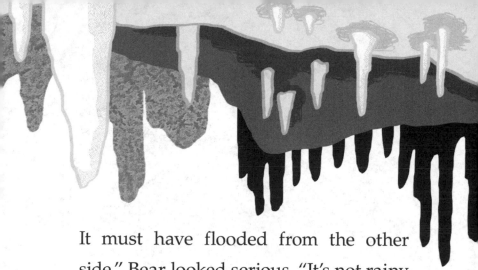

It must have flooded from the other side." Bear looked serious. "It's not rainy season yet, but a survivor always has to expect the unexpected, Harry."

"The water's rising!" Harry gasped.

Bear nodded.

Harry's heart thudded. He thought again of those millions of tons of rock between him and the open air. With water plugging up the only exits they had.

"You mean … we're trapped?"

6

HARRY'S CAVERN

"Not quite," Bear said immediately. "If water's coming in, that means air is getting out. Otherwise air pressure would hold the water back. So, if the air can find a way out then so can we."

Harry peered up the tunnel ahead of them.

"You said you got here through this pool – so, you haven't been up the tunnel that way?" he asked.

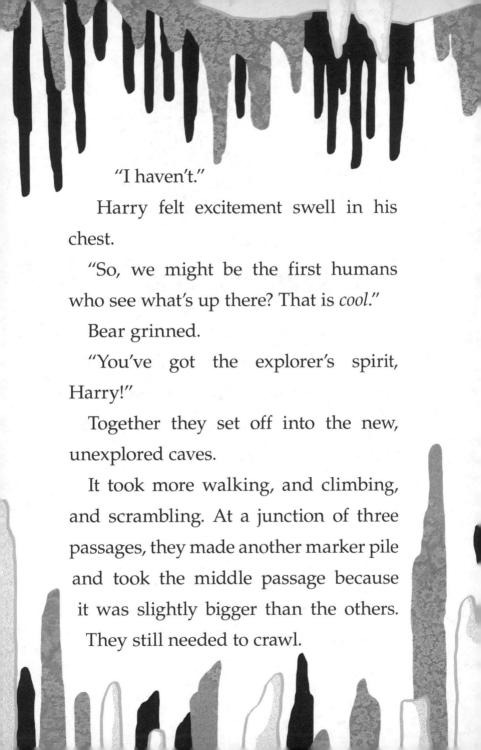

"I haven't."

Harry felt excitement swell in his chest.

"So, we might be the first humans who see what's up there? That is *cool*."

Bear grinned.

"You've got the explorer's spirit, Harry!"

Together they set off into the new, unexplored caves.

It took more walking, and climbing, and scrambling. At a junction of three passages, they made another marker pile and took the middle passage because it was slightly bigger than the others.

They still needed to crawl.

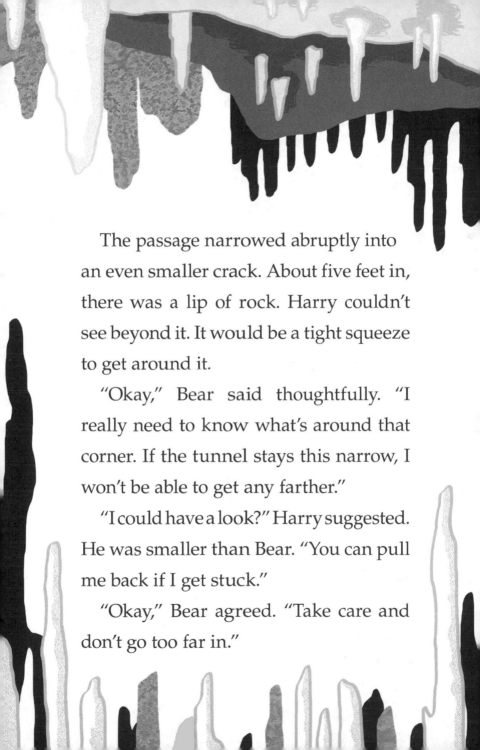

The passage narrowed abruptly into an even smaller crack. About five feet in, there was a lip of rock. Harry couldn't see beyond it. It would be a tight squeeze to get around it.

"Okay," Bear said thoughtfully. "I really need to know what's around that corner. If the tunnel stays this narrow, I won't be able to get any farther."

"I could have a look?" Harry suggested. He was smaller than Bear. "You can pull me back if I get stuck."

"Okay," Bear agreed. "Take care and don't go too far in."

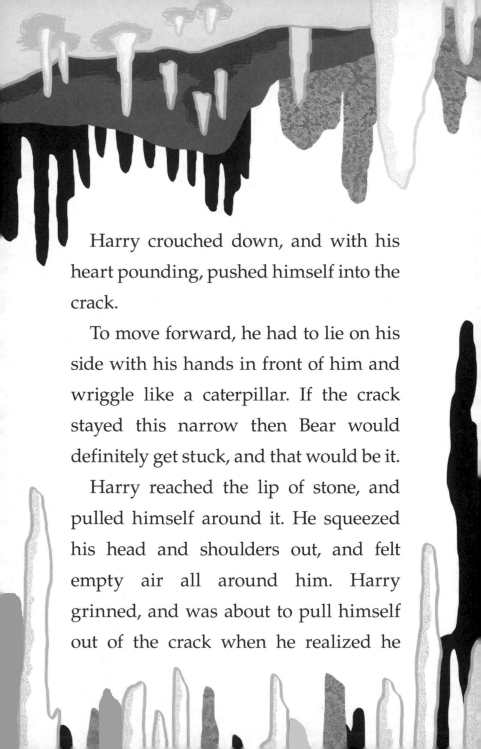

Harry crouched down, and with his heart pounding, pushed himself into the crack.

To move forward, he had to lie on his side with his hands in front of him and wriggle like a caterpillar. If the crack stayed this narrow then Bear would definitely get stuck, and that would be it.

Harry reached the lip of stone, and pulled himself around it. He squeezed his head and shoulders out, and felt empty air all around him. Harry grinned, and was about to pull himself out of the crack when he realized he

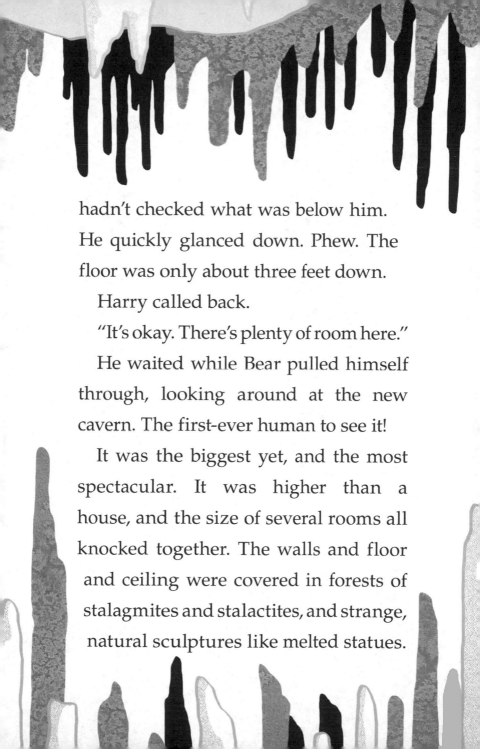

hadn't checked what was below him. He quickly glanced down. Phew. The floor was only about three feet down.

Harry called back.

"It's okay. There's plenty of room here."

He waited while Bear pulled himself through, looking around at the new cavern. The first-ever human to see it!

It was the biggest yet, and the most spectacular. It was higher than a house, and the size of several rooms all knocked together. The walls and floor and ceiling were covered in forests of stalagmites and stalactites, and strange, natural sculptures like melted statues.

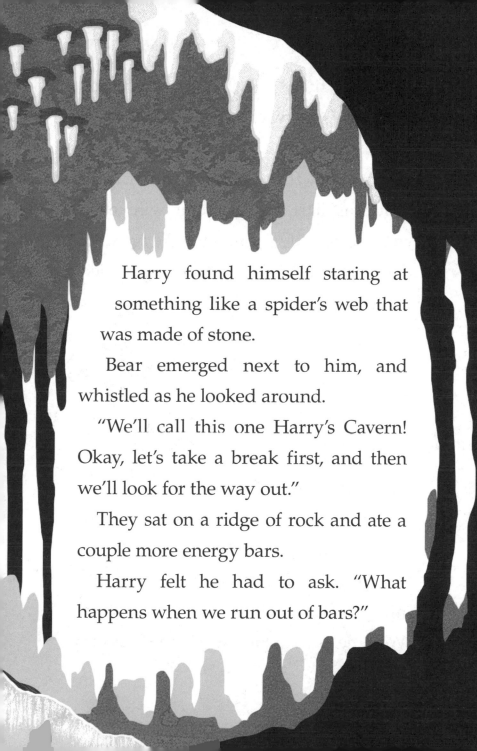

Harry found himself staring at something like a spider's web that was made of stone.

Bear emerged next to him, and whistled as he looked around.

"We'll call this one Harry's Cavern! Okay, let's take a break first, and then we'll look for the way out."

They sat on a ridge of rock and ate a couple more energy bars.

Harry felt he had to ask. "What happens when we run out of bars?"

"We'll find food," Bear told him. Suddenly, he reached up to the rocky wall behind Harry. He was holding a … thing. Harry flinched away from it.

It was like a spider, but with even more legs, wide enough to take up all of Bear's palm. The front pair of legs ended in claws, and they all grew out of a black, armored body. A single, thin spike stuck up like a tail at its rear end.

"This little guy's a whip scorpion. He's not poisonous," Bear said, setting it down and watching it scuttle away into the shadows. "And if you don't fancy eating him, there were fish back in that cenote. We'll be okay. Now, we'll find the exit quicker if we both look. I'll go around this way, you go around that way. As long as we can see each other's lights, we won't get lost." He looked at Harry seriously. "Check the ground with every step you take, Harry. What looks like a shadow could be a hole, and you won't know how deep it is until you've fallen down it."

"We'd better make a pile by this hole," Harry pointed out. "They all look the same. We might end up going back the way we've come."

"You took the words out of my mouth!" Bear smiled.

Harry and Bear pulled some small, loose rocks into a small pile at the foot of the crack they had come out of. Then they split up to explore Harry's Cavern.

Harry went clockwise.

Harry took great care where he was putting his feet. The amazing rock formations meant there wasn't a flat surface anywhere, so he spent a lot of time looking down at his legs – and seeing just how filthy his coveralls had gotten. But instead of feeling annoyed, he just smiled to himself. There were only two choices – get out of here, dirty, or stay here forever with nice, clean gear.

No contest. Even though this cavern was amazing, the idea of seeing his friends and family again was better. He couldn't wait to get home to tell them all about it.

After every careful step, Harry moved his headlight to shine all over the walls and floor, and even up at the ceiling. There might be a hole up there, hidden by the small forest of stalactites.

In fact, he almost kept his eye on the ceiling too long. Harry took another step, looked down, and saw a crack yawning in front of him.

"Whoa!"

Harry quickly stepped back.

"Are you okay?" Bear called across the cavern. His light flashed into Harry's eyes. "Did you find something?"

"Uh – yeah, I'm fine," Harry called back. He peered into the crack. It was about three feet deep, three feet long, and two feet wide. There was a thin layer of mud and gunge at the bottom. It was a dead end. "And I haven't found anything yet," Harry added.

It was still the same when he met up with Bear five minutes later, on the other side of the cavern.

Bear bit his lip thoughtfully.

"There *will* be an exit. Remember, these caves were carved out by water. For millions of years, water was getting in and flowing out. It went out through the crack we came in. But where did it come in?"

Bear put his hands on his hips and looked around. His headlight flashed over all the nooks and crannies and

shapes in the rock that they had explored.

Bear kept on thinking out loud.

"We've been going uphill for most of the time. We must be getting close to ground level. There could even be a way out, so small we can't see it. There's one thing we haven't tried, though ..."

Bear reached up to his helmet and switched the light off.

Then, before Harry could react, Bear switched off Harry's light, too.

The whole cavern was plunged into total blackness.

7

THROUGH THE U-BEND

"Do you see anything?" Bear asked out of the darkness.

"I can't see a thing," Harry said.

There was literally *no* light. At all. Anywhere. Not a glint or a glimmer. Harry tried to think of the darkest thing he had ever known. His room at home, on a night with no moon, and the curtains drawn, in the middle of a power cut. Nope, darker than that. Colored shapes floated around in the back of his eyes, like they always did if someone turned the lights out back home. But even *they* faded away, and then there was nothing. The darkness was as solid as the rock all around them.

"Let's try something," Bear said. "Look away from my voice, and tell me if you still can't see anything."

Something very faint, pale white, moved in the corner of Harry's eye. He looked towards it and it vanished.

Harry looked away. And there it was again – in the corner of his eye.

"I *think* I can see something," he said. "Sort of. But not all the time."

"Right. Is it moving?" Bear asked.

The light moved slowly. Up. Then down.

"Uh – yes. Like it's bouncing."

"That's my watch." It was weird, but Harry thought he could hear a smile in Bear's voice. "That was just to show you how our eyes work. We are expert at picking up tiny little things in the corner of our vision. It's a leftover from when our ancestors hunted on the plains. That tiny little movement might be a saber-toothed tiger hiding in the grass. Nowadays it means we notice some things better if we don't look directly at them. Right. Are you facing my voice?"

"Uh-huh," Harry confirmed.

"I'm holding my arms out towards you. You do the same."

In the dark, they took hold of each other's elbows.

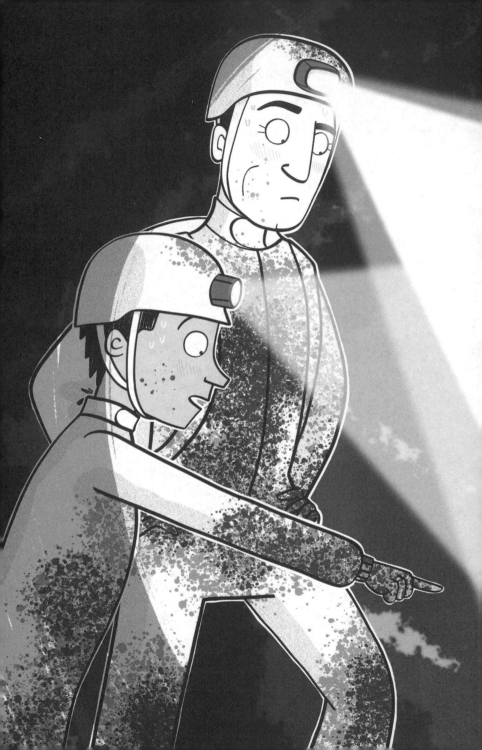

"And now," Bear said, "stare straight ahead, and we'll turn on the spot. Slowly. Clockwise. Okay, go."

They shuffled together in a slow circle.

And Harry saw a light.

It was like Bear's watch – the *tiniest* little glimmer. But only if Harry wasn't looking right at it.

Harry's heart beat with excitement.

"I see something," he said.

"Right, point at it. Then close your eyes because I'm about to turn our headlights on."

"Okay. Pointing."

Harry shut his eyes. Through his eyelids, he sensed the lights come on. He kept pointing as he opened his eyes slowly to let them adjust.

He was pointing at the crack he had nearly fallen into earlier.

Harry and Bear stood on either side of it and peered at the bottom, three feet down.

"I didn't think there was anything here," Harry said.

"Certainly looks like a dead end," Bear agreed. "But see how it bulges out a little at the bottom? It could be hiding a way out. If there's a way through under that …"

Bear lay on his front and tried to lower his top half down to peer underneath the bulge. He tried several times to get at the right angle.

Harry could see the problem. Bear would almost have to stand on his head, in a crack that was three feet deep, and only a little bit wider than Bear was. It would be very hard for him to get back up out of it.

"I can do it," Harry suggested. "I'm the right size, and if I get stuck, you can pull me out."

Bear smiled.

"Okay, nicely volunteered, mate. Let's do this."

Harry lay down on his front, then put his arms out and lowered himself vertically in. Bear held on to his feet.

Harry's hands and the top of his helmet went into the sludge at the bottom of the crack. The years of slimy mud that lined the walls of the crack covered his coveralls. Harry ignored it all and peered, upside down, under the lip of rock.

Fresh air blew very gently onto his face, and light shone down on him. Natural, yellow daylight.

"There's a way out!" he called excitedly.

"Can you get to it?" Bear called down at him.

"Yeah ... I think so ..."

Harry was lying in one half of a U-shaped tube. If he could squeeze under the lip of rock then he would come up the other side.

But then Bear was pulling him back out again.

When Harry was back on his feet, and had wiped his hands on his coveralls, which didn't make anything much cleaner, Bear asked, "Can I get to it?"

Harry had to think about that.

"Um. It's going to be tight but ... I think so, yes."

"Okay. Here's what we're going to do. I'll help you through. Then I'll push my stuff through, then I'll come myself."

Harry had a nightmare vision of Bear, wedged in the U-bend forever.

"Supposing you can't get through?" he asked.

"Sometimes you just have to take things as they come." Bear smiled. "Put it this way – I can't stay here, can I? Some things, you just don't worry about until you have to. Save your energy for later.

If I get stuck ..." He smiled again. "Then you'll just have to go for help!"

And so Bear helped Harry down again. Harry wriggled forward at the bottom of the crack. Rock scraped roughly at his coveralls and sludge slimed itself onto the fabric. His helmet grated against the sides of the crack.

But now he had the fresh air and daylight to spur him on.

With a few more kicks and wriggles, suddenly Harry was through on the other side.

"I'm through – I'm sure you can fit too!"

"On my way!" Bear called through the crack.

Harry clambered up and looked around.

And his hopes plummeted.

He was at one end of another tunnel that stretched away into the darkness. It was not as wide as Harry's Cavern, but taller. There weren't as many stalagmites or stalactites. A beam of sunlight shone down through a hole in the ceiling, onto a pile of crumbled rocks and dead leaves and vines. The hole was the size of a manhole cover.

It was almost covered with plant life, but sun and air could get through.

But the ceiling was twelve feet above Harry.

There was absolutely no chance of climbing up to it.

8

STONE STATUE

"Can you take my things, Harry?" Bear called.

First, Bear pushed his helmet through the crack.

"What about your head?" Harry called back, remembering how much it had hurt when he hit his own head.

"It's a calculated risk, Harry. This is so narrow that I can't afford anything that might get me stuck. So I'll just have to be careful of my head. Backpack coming next."

Harry pulled the bag as soon as it came through. And then he waited. The sound of scrapes and scuffles told him that Bear was squeezing himself through the crack, but there was no sign of him. Harry crouched down, ready to help Bear out. He waited. The minutes felt like hours.

Finally, Bear's arms and head appeared, followed by his shoulders and then the rest of him.

"Whew!" Bear exclaimed, once he was finally standing up again. He put his helmet back on. "I don't want to do that again! So, what have we got?"

"I don't think we can get out this way," Harry said sadly, nodding at the ceiling hole. He tried to be positive. "But I guess there's a lot more tunnel to go down."

Bear went and stood in the beam of sunlight.

"I think you're right, Harry," he agreed. He reached up and grabbed one of the vines that dangled down through the hole. It snapped and fell down on top of him in a small flurry of dirt and leaves.

"These are all too thin," Bear said thoughtfully. "We've still got the rope, but we don't have any way of getting up there to anchor it … *Whoa!*"

Suddenly the air was full of dark, fluttering, furry shapes blocking out the light. Instinctively, Harry and Bear both

ducked. The creatures swarmed around the hole and then disappeared up it, like a reverse whirlpool.

"Wow!" Harry said, smiling. "Bats!"

He had studied them for a school project. They were cool. The only mammals that could fly.

Bear smiled too.

"This place is a natural shelter for them. Looks like they're all gone. I was about to say – no place to anchor the rope, so we press on."

"At least we know we're near the surface," Harry said. It was a comforting thought, after the disappointment of seeing sunlight but not being able to get up to it.

"Absolutely. Give it a few more centuries, and that roof might crumble completely. This place will become another cenote."

They were just about to start walking when Harry's eye fell on something in the pile of debris beneath the hole. Whatever this was, it caught his attention because it was obviously man-made. He bent to pick it up.

"Wow!"

It was a statue, the size of a small doll. It looked like a person, if people really looked like they did in the pictures Harry's little sister liked to draw. Arms and legs sticking straight out. Square head, full of teeth.

"Look at this, Bear!"

Bear took the statue gently and turned it over in his hands, letting out a low whistle as he looked.

"Great spotting, Harry! This was probably a sacrifice," he said. "The ancient peoples who used to live in this part of the world thought the caverns were entrances to the underworld, so they would throw offerings in for their gods. Limestone's a soft rock so it's handy for carving. When you make a sacrifice you offer nothing but the best, so whoever made this would have slaved over it for days, maybe weeks, to get it exactly right. This guy must be centuries old."

Bear handed it back.

"Cool!" said Harry. He was the first person to touch it in hundreds of years!

The statue wasn't very big. Harry thought it would make an amazing souvenir.

But then he thought of the person who had made it, like Bear had described. Taking it wouldn't be very respectful. So Harry carefully put the little figure back where he had found it, and picked up a pointy lump of limestone 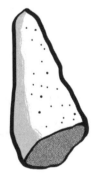 instead. It was shaped a bit like the end of a tooth, probably the tip of a fallen stalactite. One day, Harry decided, he would carve his own statue.

Then it was time to move on, away from the beam of daylight.

At first they could walk normally, but the tunnel soon began to get lower and narrower. Bear went first, and before long they were crawling again. A strange new smell was tickling Harry's nose. Something sharp that went straight to his tear ducts and made his eyes water. It was like … toilet cleaner. At least, that was what Harry's brain said it was, but he knew it couldn't be.

"I've found where the bats live," Bear said without turning around.

"Yeah?" Harry said, interested. He tried to peer around Bear. "Where are they?"

"Well, there's none here at the moment," Bear said, "but that wasn't what I was warning you about." He sounded amused. "Look down."

Harry's headlight shone down on a black, sticky layer that covered the rock in front of him. That eye-watering smell was coming from the sticky stuff.

Harry realized what he was about to crawl through.

"Yeurch! Bat poop!"

Bear chuckled.

"The technical term is 'guano,' and hey, it's a one-hundred percent natural product! Just think of it as a lot of fruit and insects ... mashed up a bit. The smell is ammonia."

Harry pulled down his sleeves to cover his hands, and kept crawling. Then his helmet clonked against the ceiling. It was getting even lower. Up ahead, Bear was now crawling on his front.

"Oh, you're kidding me!" Harry groaned.

"You can do it, Harry!" said Bear. "You've already shown loads of courage today. This is just another great opportunity for you to choose to be brave."

Harry gritted his teeth, closed his eyes and lay down on his front. Slowly he dragged himself through the revolting gunge. His eyes streamed and the fumes made him sneeze.

Sneezing made it worse because then he had to breathe in deeply. Meanwhile, the stinking, sticky mess clung to his coveralls. Harry grimaced as something cold and wet dripped down his neck and back.

After some more twists and turns, the tunnel sloped up, and then suddenly they emerged into a larger cavern. Bear high-fived him. Harry didn't bother looking down at his front. He could imagine the mess – and smell it. Instead he looked around for the next way out.

He turned a small circle, with his light flickering over the rocks.

"It's another dead end!" Harry sighed. He knew the drill. "Okay, so we turn our lights off …"

"First things first, buddy," Bear reminded him. "We haven't explored yet!"

They set off in opposite directions. Harry and Bear each found a clue at the same time.

Harry found a piece of dead wood, as long as his arm.

Bear found a pool of water.

"How did this get here?" Harry asked. He held the wood. "It couldn't have come down that crack we came through. It would've gotten stuck."

"It came through here," Bear said thoughtfully. They shone their headlights into the pool. In the clear water they could both easily see the start of a new tunnel. "It got washed through the last time this cave flooded. Hold on."

Bear reached over, and again switched off both their headlights.

This time they didn't have to try hard to see the light. It was right there in front of them.

At the other end of the flooded tunnel.

Bear turned their headlights on again and smiled at Harry.

"How long can you hold your breath, champ?" he asked.

9

BREATHE DEEP

Harry thought before he answered Bear's question. He couldn't take his eyes off the tunnel.

He was used to the caves by now. He knew how narrow passages could get as you crawled through them. It could be hard, even when you could breathe just fine.

But now he had to do it underwater. That was a whole new level of difficulty.

"Well," he said, trying to keep his voice calm, "I can swim a width of the swimming pool back at camp, underwater."

"Great!" said Bear. "That should be fine." Bear started to get the rope out. "This time, though, I'm going first. It's best if I check out the way through, in case there's anything unexpected. You hold on to this end of the rope, and once I'm through, tie the rope around your waist and I'll pull you through after me. Easy!" Bear looked confidently at Harry.

"And if I get into difficulty, you'll be able to feel it on the rope and haul me back. Okay, Harry?"

Harry had been trying to control his

worries, but the fear suddenly increased. "But what if I can't pull you out?"

Bear smiled. "It's okay. Remember, I'll be floating, so it'll be much easier than pulling me out of that crack would have been. And we managed that, didn't we? All along we've just dealt with what's in front of us, haven't we?"

Harry nodded.

"And that's all we're going to do now. We don't need to worry. We just need to move carefully but swim confidently – just like you would underwater in a swimming pool."

"Okay," said Harry, managing a half smile.

"Now, we need to get ready for this. We need to breathe slow and deep, like this. In … out …"

Harry copied Bear. The swimming instructor at camp had told him about breathing this way too. When you don't breathe, carbon dioxide builds up in your blood and makes you want to gasp for air – which would be awkward, halfway along a flooded tunnel. So the best thing to do if you were going to be underwater for a while was to get as much oxygen into your blood as possible in advance.

"That's it," Bear said. "Let your shoulders go up, stick your stomach out too, get your lungs as full as they can go."

They breathed together until Harry's head felt a bit fizzy and Bear decided they were both ready. Bear tied the rope around his waist.

"I'll give a single pull on the rope to

say I'm through. Three pulls or more means I'm in trouble and you need to get me back. Give one pull yourself when you're ready, and bring the backpack through with you – I'll need my hands free to swim, but when I'm through I can haul you on the rope and you can pull it with you. Okay, Harry?"

Harry nodded.

"See you on the other side, then!"

Bear let himself down into the pool, took one last breath and dived under.

Harry was left alone. He'd not noticed before, but it was so quiet in the cave. He let the rope pay out through his fingers as Bear swam through the tunnel. All he could hear was his own breathing. How long would this take? A minute? Two? How long could he hold his breath?

Harry told himself to think about more positive things. Like the fact that the way out of these caves was just a few feet away! He knew that he'd be glad to see the last of them, but he was also glad he had done it.

Harry looked down at himself. Wow, he was totally filthy! Mud and limescale and bat poop. He thought of his clothes under the coveralls. They were probably ruined by now with grime that must have soaked through. He grinned. For the first time ever, Harry didn't care what he looked like. So what? He had helped Bear get through the caves by being brave and working hard, not because of what style of outfit he was wearing.

The helmet and coveralls and boots weren't stylish, but they had protected him from knocks and scrapes. They were grimy and battered, but Harry wasn't. They had protected him. That was all that really mattered, Harry thought.

Just then, the rope twitched in his fingers, once.

Bear had made it!

Harry quickly tied the rope around his waist, took another few deep breaths, and eased into the cool water. He filled his lungs one last time, gave the rope a tug, gripped the backpack to his chest and dived under. The water roared and whooshed and gurgled in his ears. Almost immediately he felt himself moving forward as Bear pulled the rope in. Harry bumped and scraped along the tunnel, his helmet taking most of the knocks.

And then he was out!

When Harry broke through the surface Bear was crouched on a rock. "Great, Harry!" he said. "I'm really proud of you."

Harry just grinned and sucked clean air into his lungs.

Looking around, he could see that behind Bear was a short passage that sloped upward like a tilted chimney. Behind it, at the far end, Harry could see sunlight.

When he'd finally gotten his breath back, he leaned back and shouted with glee.

"We made it!"

Bear laughed and cheered. "Yup! Just a short climb from here."

Bear helped Harry out of the water, and

coiled the rope up around his shoulders. Bear led the way up the chimney on his hands and knees. Harry crawled after him, out into sunlight. They were in a small hollow, a few feet deep, with steep sides. Tall jungle trees towered over them in every direction.

"One more little obstacle – no problem," Bear said. He tied a loop in the end of the rope, and threw it up to lasso a boulder on the rim of the hollow. He tugged at it to check it was holding firm, then walked up the slope, pulling himself hand over hand.

Bear grinned down at Harry.

"Now, you do the same, and we are well and truly out!"

"I'm coming!"

Before he grabbed the rope, Harry

instinctively wiped his hands on his coveralls to clean them. After the wiping, they were even more filthy – covered with guano. Harry smiled, cleaned his hands as best he could on the rocks and grabbed the rope. He went up the rock face the same way Bear had done, gripping on to the rope as he powered up with his legs. At the top, Bear reached out a hand, but as Harry stretched towards it, his boots slipped. His feet shot backward and he landed with a thump on his front.

"Hey, Harry! You okay?"

"Ow!" Harry laughed. "Yeah, I'm fine..."

He pushed himself up on his arms, stared at the ground, and stopped.

This wasn't the cave, or the jungle.

He was on a platform made out of wooden slats.

Harry's head whipped around.

The person talking wasn't Bear.

Harry was lying on the wooden platform on the playground at camp. No jungle. No hollow. No Bear. The Frisbee game on the soccer field had just come to the end of another quarter.

"Come on!" George urged. "It's our turn again!"

10

BETTER THAN BAT POOP

There wasn't time for Harry to work out what was going on.

The teams were running to take their places and the ref was waiting to begin.

Harry wasn't wearing filthy caving coveralls or a helmet that squashed his hair. He was wearing his sports gear and he still had the compass zipped away in his pocket. He raced after George onto the field.

The ref checked her watch and blew her whistle for the next quarter to start. The Yellow team was ahead, so the Reds took the first throw.

George was the first to catch the Frisbee. He chucked it towards Harry, but it started to curve away towards Lily, a girl on the other team.

Harry ran hard after it, his feet pounding on the grass.

"Aargh!" he bellowed as he reached Lily just before she caught it. She flinched and Harry snatched the Frisbee.

He passed it on, and it zigzagged down the field through two more players. Suddenly the Red team had scored to equalize.

But Harry couldn't celebrate the goal. He'd grabbed the Frisbee by scaring Lily away. He felt bad.

The game started up again and the Frisbee went back and forth and around the field. No one scored for several minutes and it was still a tie as the end of the quarter approached.

A girl on the Yellow team had the

Frisbee. She had a choice of people to pass it to, all calling for it. Harry was guarding one of them. Between her and Harry there was a big, wet patch of mud.

The Frisbee raced through the air towards the player Harry was guarding.

Harry charged straight across the muddy patch, eyes on the Frisbee. He felt the mud splash up onto his socks and legs and shorts, but he didn't care. He leaped up and grabbed the Frisbee out of the air, landed, and chucked it to George, all in one movement. George flicked it into the goal, a moment before the ref blew her whistle to mark the end of the game, and a Red team victory.

"They thought you wouldn't run to catch it there," George laughed as they celebrated. "You're covered in mud now!"

Harry grinned. The rush and buzz of the Frisbee game had pushed the whole cave adventure to the back of his mind, but suddenly he was reminded of all the dirt and danger. He couldn't explain it, but here he was. It had to have been some kind of weird dream, but even so, he knew that he had learned a lot from it.

"Well," Harry said, "it's better than being covered in bat poop!"

Now it was George's turn to look puzzled.

"Um – I guess."

Harry smiled. Then he noticed Lily,

standing on her own, looking sad. He felt bad again.

He hated people who threw their weight around to get what they wanted. And that had been exactly what he'd done when he'd frightened Lily and snatched the Frisbee.

Harry walked over to her.

"Hi, Lily. Listen … um … I'm sorry if I scared you back there. I really didn't mean to."

"It's okay," Lily said. "I know you didn't. It's hard to stand my ground sometimes."

"Right …" Harry didn't really know what to make of that. "Still friends?"

"Oh … yes." Lily smiled. "Still friends."

Harry felt a bit better.

As they left the field, Harry wished

he could help Lily, to make up for scaring her. Then he felt the compass with five directions in his pocket.

He pulled it out. It had just the usual four directions now – North, South, East, West. His mind really was doing strange things today.

Harry felt something else in his pocket, solid and heavy.

Frowning and puzzled, he took it out.

A piece of pale-yellow rock. Limestone. Pointed, like the end of a tooth, but smooth. Perfect for carving a statue out of.

Harry stared at it.

How did that get there?

Somehow, this limestone rock had found its way back from his dream about the cave.

The cave was real! It *couldn't* have been a dream. So was everything that went with it. Bear and the adventure had been real – and he'd learned so much.

What did the compass and its five directions have to do with it all? Harry took it out and looked at it again. Was this what started it? Could it do it again? Could the compass help Lily have an adventure and learn something too?

Harry looked up.

"Hey, Lily!"

Lily sighed.

"Harry. Look, it's really okay, I'm fine …"

"No, it's not that," he assured her.

Harry held out the compass.

"I, um, thought you might like this?" he said. "Just consider it a gift."

The End

Bear Grylls got the taste for adventure at a young age from his father, a former Royal Marine. After school, Bear joined the Reserve SAS, then went on to become one of the youngest people ever to climb Mount Everest, just two years after breaking his back in three places during a parachute jump.

Among other adventures he has led expeditions to the Arctic and the Antarctic, crossed oceans and set world records in skydiving and paragliding.

Bear is also a bestselling author and the host of television programs such as *Survival School* and *The Island*.

He has shared his survival skills with people all over the world, and has taken many famous movie stars and sports stars on adventures – and even President Barack Obama!

Bear Grylls is Chief Scout to the UK Scouting Association, encouraging young people to have great adventures, follow their dreams and to look after their friends. Bear is also honorary Colonel to the Royal Marine Commandos.

When Bear's not traveling the world, he lives with his wife and three sons on a barge in London, or on an island off the coast of Wales.

Find out more at **www.beargrylls.com**